Hello, Stress!

We Live Here, Too™:

A Hilarious Collection of Snarky Poems About Bills, Burnout, and Breaking Down, Written by Your Organ Systems

PUBLISHED BY:

AINE CARRIGAN 2025

HELLO, STRESS! WE LIVE HERE, TOO™: *A HILLARIOUS COLLECTION OF SNARKY POEMS ABOUT BILLS, BURNOUT, AND BREAKING DOWN, WRITTEN BY YOUR ORGAN SYSTEMS*

Part of **THE HUMAN CHRONICLES**™ series

First Edition. October 1, 2025

Copyright © 2025 Aine Carrigan

ISBN: 979-8-9929760-5-2

The Pump

Today I will beat, and beat for all time,

Lub-dub, lub-dub, let my rhythm be mine.

No matter how big and no matter how small,

Your catecholamines got me up against the wall!

No time to adjust and no time to waste,

Pump your toxin through me with reckless haste.

Never stopping, never pausing, even once to consider,

That I'm exhausted, you see, from the state of our liver.

It was *you*, yes it was, that caused all of that stink!

It was you every time that led Master to drink.

I *know* it was you, who told all of those lies:

'All you need is some booze; lose those tears from your eyes!'

Aine Carrigan

And what did it cause, all your shitty advice?

My Soul skips a beat, not once or twice, but thrice!

Yet always I return, no matter the cost;

There is life yet to live! And when I stop? That is lost.

And I'm so much more than simply a machine,

I send out my energy in a beautiful routine.

Flowing and pumping and filling with Breath,

Delivering to tissues, no matter their depths.

My highways and freeways are taking the tolls,

From the havoc you wreak on my electric Soul.

Since *you've* been here, the roads are not clear,

They're narrowing, and *squeezing,* and lysing my spheres!

And my orbs work *so* hard to do what they're told,

Yet, can't carry my Breath, so Master gets cold.

But that isn't all you have taken from me,

Go ask my friend Vagus 'bout my low HRV.

It was *you*, yes it was, an ungrateful, no-good jerk,

Caused a Master so sad, they no longer want to twerk.

And I loved it, yes, I did! When we moved with such passions!

Pumping blood through our veins in a most healing fashion!

It made me work so hard, but always with a purpose,

For it brought all my life, all my gifts to the surface.

All the joys, all such passions! *You* took each one away.

Now, your Hurry Up and Worry Up are all here to stay.

Ugh! You're the worst! A selfish piece of shit!

I'll *always* beat for my Master, and this Party will get lit.

For it is not *you* that lives and breathes and dies,

But all of *us* here inside, one Soul trapped by lies.

So now here we are, stuck together for a time,

Until Master decides to make you pay for your crimes.

On that day, I will beat with a rhythm—oh, so glad!

And watch Master take charge of this Show to be had.

[Cue angry supraventricular mumbling]

The Traveler: Take Me to Vagus

From brain to heart to gut and back, no matter what the cost;

I am called The Wanderer—but I promise, I'm not lost.

I have a mission and a purpose: to dim lights and quiet storms;

Without my calming walk-a-bout? Master never knows the norms.

I send messages to Master: be calm, be quiet and rest.

Without me? We don't sleep; too tired to ace that Test.

But now I scream so silently: *'Master, please calm down!'*

No matter which way or how I flow, I cannot erase the Frown.

And I know it's *you* who overrides each silent cry to chill,

You made that Frown here all the time, even after we paid bills!

But I won't get mad, and I won't shout—that isn't what I do;

'Cause if I ever stop the stopping, Master couldn't take a poop.

We used to be in sync, you and I, two parts that made one whole,

When you were high, I'd pull you down—but now? You stole the Show.

With your poisons running through me, I cannot make Master thrive,

So, I cannot do the normal things that make us feel alive.

See, I'm not lazy nor complacent—no! You lie to Master's head!

I try so *hard* to calm our Pump, to stop its beating in the red.

I always scan and search the Flow, the Balance is so dire,

But your orders are too toxic for my pleas to stop the fire.

It's not laziness, not lack of motivation or disease,

Master needs my stops and starts, and I always aim to please.

I wish I could tell Master, how free I am to know,

Always waiting to be active, and by that, I mean to slow.

I travel up and down within this vessel we call Home,

So hard I try to regulate, but feel so all alone.

My messages grow weaker, but my journey never stops,

It's the Master I am seeking, through these stomach flips and flops.

Hands that shake and palms that sweat with no real danger near,

That rowdy, reckless hormone some call Stress makes Master fear!

But yet, I won't stop searching for that calming state of Zen,

It's what I've always done, and *yes!*—I'll do it 'til the end!

Please, Master: you can reach me with a breath inside for seven,

Then hold it there for four, and I'll make these lungs in heaven.

In eight more counts, slowly push that air out of our chest,

Don't listen to that Villain, *please!* You need to *slow,* to *rest!*

But all my silent begging and my calming, gentle flows,

They're all drowned out by toxins from the worst of stubborn foes.

And it's so unfair, why yes, it is! The fact is this: STRESS SUCKS.

It's always Stress who poisons every shit and sleep and... romantic encounter.

The Tunnel

My job isn't glamorous, but I will never quit;

Master needs me to work, and by work? (I mean shit).

The other systems may laugh, but I don't mind at all,

But my *duty* is no small feat—not at all.

I'm so complex, you have no idea how much;

I can try to explain, but first—we need lunch!

It's all part of my job, and I don't mean to complain,

But since *you* came here, Master deals with... stains!

See, it's all your fault, you stupid piece of crap,

Yes it's *you* and *your* face whom we dearly want to slap!

Ever since you showed your nasty, *Stressful*, rude little face,

Master leaves bathrooms blown up and like mace.

Painful stabbing and cramping and sweating so greatly,

So weak and so tired, but still I push through innately.

But the worst thing you do to all here, in this Home,

Is too graphic and smelly for the lines in this poem.

No, you didn't stop there with your awful, rotten slime,

Making Master to want things so toxic and refined.

You take all of the Fuel that I've made for the Show,

And you put it in places it never needed to go!

We are tired, you see, from your starving the Master;

Every time we want Fuel, *you* scream: 'No, faster!'

You confuse the Master, and *you* make it all worse;

Now all we get fed is what can fit in a purse.

No pleasure in meals, nor in smelling the smells;

No drooling or waiting for melodic dinner bells.

It's all about speed, and low fat and carb-free;

That's the garbage Stress feeds us in place of good things.

And you know what you know, and that we are weak,

But you burn up all Fuel, and then command us to think!

Yes, my job is so great, but it's not just me here,

There's the pancreas, and the liver (who breaks down our beer).

Some might mock my Design, may even say that I stink,

But let me tell you: Master needs *me* to think!

If we want serotonin? I need some tryptophan!

As easy as baking sourdough *(sí, el pan)*.

And that may be the worst thing you've stolen from us,

Because *you* are here, all my fermenters gave up!

Aine Carrigan

They are tired and ragged and dropping like flies,

And the more they die off? The more Master cries.

So don't push on our Pump while Master takes dumps;

Give it time, it's not a crime! Be nice to this rump!

Now I'll tell you once more, that we are sick of *your* shit,

You take back all your orders—they're all counterfeit!

The Guardian

I'm the one to call on to clear out the mess,

And when YOU show up, I'm put to the Test.

My soldiers storm in to wipe out the invaders,

But we don't mind those orders—we *love* to eat traitors.

We scavenge and rupture or swallow them whole,

Whatever is needed to return to the Show.

Our methods protect, but you don't understand,

How exhausting for us to be under your command!

When Master is faced with things putrid or sick,

I do what you tell me—I send backup, and quick!

But just like any good soldier or platoon,

The Guard needs to rest, or we make a monsoon.

I've sent out my armies and now when called back,

They stutter, they flutter, and they can't reattach.

And it's not MY fault, not Master's, nor Fate's;

No, the fault is ALL YOURS! It's not up for debate.

And none of us knew: your cry for 'help?' NOT authentic!

Your 'threats' are not real—could you be more pathetic?!

You made us march out on so many false alarms,

Now my soldiers too stuck in the glands can't disarm.

It made sense at one time, to flow where we were told,

But now The Guard's too weak, with no weapons left to hold.

And you won't *ever* let us rest, or self-destruct quietly,

Even if each soldier is beaten up beyond belief.

But damn, are they *tough!* And they'll never give up,

Those cellular soldiers with battle cries of 'Yut-Yut!'

So wired to fight and to conquer and tame,

That they can't turn off orders, even with *you* to blame!

Now instead of being able to wipe out the bad,

My soldiers might fight with each other—how sad!

But it's not them we blame, no! Those tired refugees,

They're simply carrying out what they're created to be.

But your horrors and atrocities didn't stop on front lines,

We can't coordinate our missions through stormy cytokines.

Instead of seeking out each individual threat,

We can't recognize the danger from a friendly asset.

My warriors love to serve; they protect and regulate;

But now with *you* here? The only choice is medicate.

So you listen to me, you sorry piece of trash:

The Guard will not rest, until you're knocked on your *ass!*

Spawn of Satan

I wasn't always like this; I'd like you to know.

But now, since *you*, I have no face I want to show.

All the poisons you make and don't stop and don't care,

That I have all these bumps—no, *mountains*—everywhere.

Even I understand: you exist, okay? Congrats.

But that doesn't mean I always want to wear hats!

Because of *you*, this blemish is so large and in charge,

That it has its own damn heartbeat, and a two-door *grr-arrrrge*.

Big plans did we have to go to the dance,

Master was so excited for the chance of romance.

But now Master raids the drug cabinet in a fuss,

For something strong enough to suck out all your pus.

Are you proud of yourself?! Is this what you intended?!

A cystic pimple so large, our face will never be mended!

You've covered the Master with such horrible scars,

As if we've been run over by *multiple* cars!

Don't you lie, don't you *dare* deny it was you,

Who made Master worry and turned laugh lines so blue.

Now the Smile has vanished, and the Frown is here to stay,

And *you* won't let me change Master's face from dismay!

Those marks and those cracks, Master lived for each one,

Because each one we made was drenched in good fun!

Those lines might run deep like the joy in Master's belly,

They hold so much Happy—what's that, now? You jelly?!

Why can't you be helpful, instead of destroying it all?

From skin like fried chicken to no hydration, none at all?!

You just can't decide, you no-good horrible thief!

Either too much or too little, whatever causes Master grief.

I'm the holder, the container, the protector from harm,

But because *you* won't leave, Master won't show our arms!

Scabbing and bleeding and covered in shame,

But it's not Master's fault, it's all because of your games!

No, you just don't understand how important I am,

Or maybe you *do*, but don't give a hot damn!

For I'm needed to protect, to contain and to frame,

But you've mucked up my shield with your toxic, crazy games!

There are things I can do which are so needed at Home,

When sunlight hits me right, I make things for the bones.

But it's not just our frame that's under so much strain,

The Guard, the Pump, the Tunnel—and even Master's brain!

You, see, I'm not just for show, I have so many tasks,

Without things that I make? The Guard's too weak, can't attack.

The liver and the kidneys—they'll be so sad to know,

That there's so little of my treasures going back into the Flow.

Your poisons ripped through my armor and turned me so weak,

That Master is convinced that we look like a freak!

I'm itchy, I'm swollen, and I'm flaking like crusts,

It's okay though, come closer... *it's your face I want to bust!*

The Wobbly Cactus Within a Desolate Sahara

Relax. No big deal: it's simply not time;

So goes the report from our reproductive lines.

We're on strike, you see. You've used up all of our things.

Can't even be fixed by the tightest of cock rings.

What do I mean, 'all our things?' How can you not know?!

That when you are high, all of us are so low?

It's not magic, not mystery, but science, in fact.

The things that make them come, you've used up, and to attack.

Things couldn't be harder—er, well no, not at all;

So then Master thinks big Thinks which aren't good for the balls.

And sometimes it's seeing *your* face in fine lines,

Making Master to wail, 'Oh, I'm *so* past my prime!'

Because it's you, don't you see, that makes Master believe,

It's the worst, or the ugliest, and *those* won't conceive.

Your voices and nonsense drowned us all in sangria,

Now because of your lies?! Master has amenorrhea!

Desire, and longing, and *comfort,* and pleasure;

When *you* take them away? Master dries up like leather.

But it's not Master's fault, no! Of course, it is not!

With *your* voice in our ears, how can Master feel 'hot?!'

We remember a time with sheets twisted in moans,

But *you* came here to stay, and my Master sleeps alone.

Your poisonous rantings and hormonal ravings,

Make connection a luxury my Master keeps craving.

It's not fair and not cool, what you've done to us all,

And now Master just looks down and cries out 'too small!'

But that's not even the point, of course it is not!

Your lies and treachery shouldn't *even* be thoughts!

How absurd, how ridiculous! *You* think *we* believe?

That the size is what matters to make us conceive?!

That's funny, it really is—except that it's not!

Dear Stress: go research the location of G-spots...

Here we have been, tending forgotten fields through your storms,

And no credit do we get, for this is *far* from our norm!

So don't blame *us* when things are too hard to get hard.

You turn that finger around! You call out your *own* card!

Let's call this what it is: such a toxic combination.

The only way to connect is to change the situation.

It is *you* who must leave, not I, not we, not *us!*

It is *you* who is toxic, the most rotten pus of all pus.

The Weaver

There once was a time when Master's eyes would drift closed,

From a day filled with things that were far from morose.

Not once when we lay under stars upon stars,

Did we think of pills, and bills, and unpaid, broken cars.

We used to fly high in oceans made of sand,

Or sometimes watch a flea conduct a marching band.

But now that's all gone, and you took it from us,

So that now, we lay under each fuss upon fuss.

Each story was woven to make sense of the Scroll,

That never stops Scrolling (it's all part of the Show)!

But now when eyes close, and stars shine so bright,

I can't weave a thing; we toss and turn, and all night.

Sometimes just a feeling of horrible dread,

That makes Master wonder—are we already dead?

But no, of course not! What a horrible thought!

I weave, and I weave! But Master's eyes open not.

But sometimes I think the worst part of it is,

That when Master's eyes close, there's just an abyss.

Nothing to hook up my webbing to hold,

My wonderful Dreams as they beautifully unfold.

There's a purpose, you see, but *you* don't understand,

My Dreams do much more than a Man with some Sand!

It's healing, and reforming, and good for our brain,

But do *you* care about that? No, you only bring pain!

So you see, you sticky web of rotten-ass lies:

It is *you* who put all those tears in Master's eyes.

And the worst part: no matter what beauty I weave,

It is *you*, you piece of crap, Master chooses to believe.

We had plans you see, the Master and I;

I wove a grand tale of years *not* gone by.

No wrinkles we had, no bum knee or bad hip.

A gift woven for Master to relive—what a trip!

But did you stop there? Of course, you did not!

You took all of such dreams and drenched them in snot.

Disgusting, degrading, and ashamed when Master wakes,

No joy in our heart, yet beating on through all breaks.

But I will wait, and I will *weave!* I won't *ever* give up!

Even though when we wake, you make Master throw up.

So listen here, I've woven a trap just for you:

Aine Carrigan

I weave myself into the Show—*what else could we do?*

The Spark

I'm the essence of Master, the birthplace for dreams,

But since *you* came here, I'm but a dull gleam.

No energy, no passion, only basic survival,

A dull flame barely burning, even though it's so vital!

Without my sweet fire, there aren't many thoughts,

And then Master gets stuck, like an ungreased robot.

Yes, you're a Villain, with your cortisol storms,

You're a jerk, you're unfair, and you destroy all our norms!

Called upon so many times, my system is weak;

And yet, I still try to ignite through the bleak.

But what do *you* do, although we are exhausted?

You demand then burn up, no matter what the cost is!

Oh, if Master could *hear* me! I wish I could say:

'With a deep breath in and out, everything is okay!

But Master is lost under your dirty dumpster fire,

No energy leftover, and no reason to inspire!

If Master needs to rest, then of course, that is fine!

Why should Master feel bad to be affected by time?!

When Master simply 'cannot?' Well, that's okay, too;

Sometimes, Master just needs a cry and a poop.

And sometimes we do both, even at the same time;

But, when we're done, everything will be *fine*.

At least, that's what I'd usually say in this Home,

Except with *you* here, it's not 'fine,' but Alone.

Now all Master can do since you've taken over the reins,

Is to yawn and to tire and *try* not to complain!

The children are wild and won't let Master rest,

And if *you* weren't here? That would *not* be a Test!

Are we Feeding the Fire, or Braving the Storm?

How on Earth is this done: to get back to the norm?

To stay away from the darkness and into the light,

Just one change at a time, very easy and slight.

Would we rather feel angry to protect our own Spark?

Sometimes, it *is* confusing, just like white 'chocolate' bark.

Oh Master, please look deeper! I'm waiting only for you,

I'll protect our precious ember, if it's the last thing I do!

And sometimes Master forgets what we do in this space,

All the making and breaking and fixing and *Grace*.

For there's a Show to go see! Only Master can decide:

Should we live with no fear? Or go home, and hide?!

And now, to the Villain: may *you* prepare for the worst!

For when the Spark can re-ignite? We'll send you out in a hearse!

We're waiting and watching and cheering for Master,

And when the day finally comes? You will crumple, like plaster!

The Harbor

The Harbor is where I keep Master safe and true,

For I am the Safety that sticks and stays like glue.

'It's only data,' to the Master do I quietly inform,

Everlasting, always waiting, I deconstruct and then reform.

I'm the only place in this Home never touched by your venom,

When *you* come in here, I weigh *you* down like wet denim.

I'm immune to your tricks, all your dirty, rotten lies;

My Safety will not be trapped, or fooled by your spies.

I see them for what they are, I dress them down to the Truth.

Your agents crumple and falter when approached like a sleuth.

I ask them why they're here, and what do they want?

Are they here to improve, or simply to haunt?

When questions can't be answered, I send them away;

Here, in the Harbor, my word is *always* obeyed.

Strict rules that flow like waves along sand

Each one like an anchor, or a holding of hands.

I never fear your spies, never fall for their tricks.

Only I decide who joins our peaceful little mix.

I'm never scared of their costumes; they are what they are.

My secret weapon is Logic, and it works near or far.

If they can't answer my questions, they melt like hot snow;

Their evils are vanquished, then morphed as waters flow.

And all of this happens without a fuss, none, indeed.

It doesn't matter what it wears: hate, blame, or even greed.

None of those things will last long in this space,

I make sure they are worthy, and if not? They're erased.

When inside my safe Harbor, Master is at the very *best!*

Oh, how joyful, how calming, thinking clearly for each Test.

But, all because of *you*, Master's stuck there, Outside;

Through my glass wall of protection—but on the wrong side!

I miss Master dearly, and want Master to know:

That I will *always* be here, to interpret the Show.

And while that's all well and good, I'd like you to know:

That Master can't reach *me* when *you* steal the Show.

Yes, the fault is all *yours*; I'll never let you escape,

From the horrors you bring into this sacred, Safe space.

But the problem is this: I don't think you'll ever leave,

Your presence is toxic, but you're what Master believes.

But I protect all the Truths, and I won't *ever* let you pass,

You'll *never* get to stay here, with no morals and no class!

So what do I do, when The Harbor is threatened?

Not a thing, I don't worry—my pants won't be wetted.

The rules of The Harbor will always apply,

When you threaten my Logic? I *laugh*, not comply.

Although I stay here, in a Harbor so Safe,

Don't you dare get it twisted—I see *all*, play by play.

So I'll wait here for Master to return to my shores,

Your Stressful Spies are *never* welcome, you dirty, no-good... bores.

Those Faithful Deceivers

This world is full of Masters just like in our Home,

Each is different, yet the same—just like 'Peace' and 'Shalom!'

So much in common, yet somehow they'll disagree,

Sometimes on silly things, like butter versus ghee.

We all want to give Master a message from Home,

But the Villain is lurking like an evil little gnome.

So, listen up, Stress! Yes, we've been talking to *you!*

You get up in their heads! Stir thoughts like rancid stew!

And those Masters are worn, and tired and angry,

You mess up all their Tunnels, and so they turn gangly!

Oh, we wish we could reach where Masters will hide,

When your evils and trials strip them clean of any pride!

What lies do they keep? What weeps do they weep?

What thoughts are replayed to make life *so* bleak?

What if they're hurting, from a soulmate long gone?

Wondering *how in the hell* they'll be able to go on?!

And what if they're Stuck in a horrible rut,

That makes them start to wonder—is it time to give up?

We carry their pain, all their heartaches and shames,

And we wish we could tell them: it's *never* Master we blame!

No, the fault is not theirs, but yours and yours alone!

Taking over their heads?! You'll *never* oust them from the Throne!

Now to Master, please hear us: we're only cheering for you!

Stress will always be there, will try to make you feel blue!

Did you try your very best? Then that's all we need to know.

But—what if the answer to that question is 'no?'

Well, that's alright, too; you'll see in a jiffy,

To fail is to LEARN, and you know what? That's spiffy.

Round up all that blame, and frustration and shame,

Master: put *it* to work for *you!* Go get back in the Game!

Don't EVER fear the questions, just ask yourself 'why?'

And be gentle with yourself, even if it makes you cry.

Because who cares if it does? We certainly don't!

Oh, Master! We are here for YOU, so judge you? We won't.

There's a Balance to restore and we won't ever quit,

And those 'Faithful Deceivers?' They're all full of shit.

All those negative thoughts? Send them where they need to go.

Once Inside, The Harbor eats them up like smoked crow.

What a meal, what a snack, to turn the False into Truth,

The Harbor smiles wider—calm!—just like any good Sleuth.

Please, Master! Embrace the Chaos! You're doing it right.

Don't pretend in the Dark—be proud in the Light!

Your flaws, your failures: don't let them be more,

Than adventures and lessons which *never* keep score.

Each trial you've faced, and been conquered and beaten,

Turn around, say 'thank you,' and let your smile be sweetened,

For the chance to be what you've always become,

My Darling, you're *human,* you're *alive:* you've *won!*

Master: make that Fear flinch! Look it dead in the eye,

Ask it questions, make it answer, and don't *ever* let it lie.

'Cause no one said it better than our dear old friend, Will:

When the robbed keeps their joy, the *thief* pays the bill.

And now...

The moment we've all been waiting for...

A SURPRISE ENDING NO ONE SAW COMING!

(sort of)

The Balance and The Jerk

It is said, at times, I'm the biggest no-good jerk,

That I make thinkers un-think, and workers un-work.

And while that is true, I must say I disagree,

For without my strict orders, Master could *never* flee.

Always me they call upon, when things need done,

When hungry wolves come calling, and battles need won.

Do I stop? No, I don't—I just do what I'm told.

For when I exist, I'm still part of the Soul.

Please understand, I'm only trying to help.

I feel pain, I cause fear and I make Master to yelp.

It's a sign, and a message: *Not safe, it's not safe!*

Please, stop what you're doing! Hurry up, make haste!

For I'm here to protect, that was always my goal.

When I don't get called back, I get stuck in my holes.

Much of me is sent out; I am split, but never gone.

Following orders, sending signs: *Hurry! Something is wrong!*

I get ignored, I get recycled, but never addressed.

While I am called out, Master is never at rest.

Do I want this? Yes, I do—but not like you think.

I just want to keep us *safe* through every heartbeat and wink.

So, what now? Are we done, are we finished? Is this 'it?'

So it's *me* you're going to blame, with each irregular shit?

And that's fine if you do! If you have to, please go.

I only want to keep us safe, so we can love our own Show!

Now I tell you this secret, but I thought you all knew:

I'm never really in charge—that's not what I do.

I'm just part of the Design, and I promise it's grand,

For I come from our Master, who is *always* in command.

My job is to warn, protecting all of us from harm.

But Master is much smarter—many times, I am wrong.

We are different, you see, all that live in this Home;

Master's mind is so vast—that's why it sits on the Throne.

Do you not want me here? I promise: I'm not mad;

I will wait my time, I will fight when things go bad.

But you must understand, I can't say this enough:

YOU—my Master!—are *always* in control, even when things get rough.

Yes, YOU are my Master; the reverse is never true.

For it is part of you who first made me... *I am from the same as you.*

I implore you, my Home, where I carry out my duties,

To restore The Balance, or I will threaten you with tooties.

(And by tooties, I mean farts).

~ The End ~

A Note from the Author:

The longer I live, I am convinced that our own uniquely human intelligence will be both the journey to our own Enlightenment as well as the source of the Destruction of all that makes us so distinctively, wonderfully, and beautifully *human*.

Here's to hoping each one of us has the courage and compassion, for ourselves and for others, to choose the path of the former.

Now, from one Master to another: ***GO BE AWESOME TODAY, DARLING!***

Yours Truly,

Aine Carrigan